Lawson vs. LaValley © 2012
by John Edward Lawson and Dustin LaValley

Published by Raw Dog Screaming Press
Bowie, MD

First Edition

"Actionable Intelligence" first published in *Rumble*
"The Baby Burns Eaily" first published in *A Razor Ocean*
"The Lightness of Being" first published in *The Dodsley Pages*
"Like Water For Shaivo" first published in *Blood Cookies*
"This Shit'll Put Hair On Your Chest (And In Your Stab Wound)" first
published in *Micro100*

Cover Image: Cory Galusha,
Book Design: M. Garrow Bourke

Printed in the United States of America

ISBN: 978-1-935738-21-3 (hc) /978-1-933293-18-6 (pbk)

Library of Congress Control Number: 2009939565

www.RawDogScreaming.com

LAWSON

VS.

LAVALLEY

RAW DOG
SCREAMING
PRESS

ALSO BY DUSTIN LAVALLEY

Collections
Lowlife Underdogs
The Bleeding

Illustrated
A Child's Guide to Death (with John Edward Lawson, Darin Malfi, and Mark Sullivan)

Sequential Art
Interference

Films
Party Girl
Terror Overload
You're Next 3: Pajama Party Massacre
Rise of the Ghosts (with Robbie Ribspreader)

ALSO BY JOHN EDWARD LAWSON

Novels
New Mosque City
Last Burn in Hell: Director's Cut

Collections
Discouraging at Best
Pocket Full of Loose Razorblades

Poetry
SuiPsalms
The Troublesome Amputee
The Plague Factory

Illustrated
A Child's Guide to Death (with Darin Malfi, Dustin LaValley, and
Mark Sullivan)

As Editor
Miseduction of the Writer (with Chesya Burke and Maurice Broaddus)
Tempting Disaster
Sick
Of Flesh and Hunger

John's dedication:
For Darin, Mark, Ash, and Joseph.

Dustin's dedication:
For Rob Tongue, Tim Costin, Mark Sullivan, and Richard Nicol.

CONTENTS

ROUND
1

IN THIS CORNER...

Dustin LaValley

YEARS BACK, WHEN it dawned on me that I had begun writing for more than a hobby, for eyes, views and imaginations other than my own, I picked up a few books on the art of writing. Most were bullshit. But there were one or two that came through and scattered throughout the puffery I found some advice that has stuck with me. In practice and time, I found a place for myself. For my writing and, I felt comfortable. The work I produced was named, clothed and housed. And that house kept filling, brothers and sisters, cousins and friends. As the stories came out on an evermore consistent basis they began, like children, to mature and travel further apart from the others. They didn't have genres, they had hints and hues but never assigned to any specific category. And that to me is great, as that is what I set out to do. I don't believe in finding your voice. I believe in finding your voices, which makes collections such as this difficult to compile, as there is no set merger, no connection between the stories. They're their own cultures, societies and worlds. I support each and every as I support the other, I take no favorites. Well, sometimes. Just like parents do, though they will never tell the children... Or at least shouldn't tell the children. The voices may create worlds of torment and bloodshed, whispers and shadows or smiles inside subtle darkness. The polished, edited product is when I know the temperament of the piece. Never during creation, as it could change at any time on a whim.

The stories presented here are dark, humorous and vulgar at times yet at the same, they may be symbolic of society, perhaps a suggestion in metaphor pertaining to and of cultural norms and a dose of the creator's own individual views can be noticed. There is always more to what is on the page, the words and worlds and their characters left to be tossed and turned in the mind of the reader. What is taken from each story by each reader may never be the same, one will identify differently than the other. This carries on into each writer's own personal style of creation. It's possible, though doubtful, the stories produced by my opponent (the bully he is, picking a fight with a man who has half the reach) may spark your interest more so than my own... And if they do, that's perfectly all right but I will tell you now that if that is the fact, we can not be friends. And if you side with me, if you chant my name and stand beside me when challenged by a pompous punk such as John Edward Lawson, then our future is bright and I look forward to our friendship.

Bruised and bloody,
Dustin LaValley

THIRTEEN MILKMEN
Dustin LaValley

WHEN I HAD heard that Mr. Woodrow had passed away, I was not surprised. The man had been suffering for some time, all along wearing a smile and keeping a spring in his step. It was cancer. It's always cancer. Slowly it ate away at him and the whole time he denied treatment, saying if he was going to go, he was going to go and that couldn't be changed. That he wasn't going to be pumped with strange and harmful chemicals. I have to hand it to him, he was quite the trooper. When he didn't show up for his route, and those who still used the assistance of a Milkman noticed there were no fresh bottles on their doorsteps that morning, worries grew as it was no secret Mr. Woodrow was ill. When his boss phoned his house and there was no answer, the police were called. They had broken down the door and found the old man, dressed in his freshly pressed white suit, black shoes and black bowtie on the floor face down, just a few feet from the front door. Quite the trooper he was.

Mrs. Waters was on his route, and when I learned this through the rumor mill about town, I instantly made it my business to befriend the Milkman. The widow, Mrs. Waters was pleasant and easy on the eyes, very easy on the eyes. And though she was a woman and had the natural failings that all women have, the generous life insurance payout her late husband had left in his wake made up for such faults. If I wasn't taken by her beauty, I was taken by her money... the latter more so.

But therein lies the problem. I was not alone in my pursuit of the widow, Mrs. Waters. Twelve, yes, twelve other men had taken up romancing the woman. Some would like to believe that their infatuation was purely drawn by the powers of attraction between a man and woman, but I knew that at heart they were just like me. There was Jack Speegle, Shaun Thomas, Jonathon Strand, Jeffery Lawson, Garry Staley, Chuck Charles, Stephen Keene, Brian Crowther, Mort King, Ed White, Ray Little and Bentley Lee. The twelve suitors that stood between me and the rich widow would prove to be most difficult but I, Sir, am no coward and am not deterred that easily.

And I haven't mentioned it yet I believe, but my plan, though seemingly genius and creative, had not been as original as I had thought when conceived. I was to disguise myself as the new Milkman and through my thrice weekly deliveries seduce the widow, Mrs. Waters, and before you could say "Jack-Shit," she and her millions would be mine. If you're thinking: *Why did he take the risk disguising himself instead of going for the job?* The reason is the delivery of milk is a dead language. Almost no one has milk delivered anymore with all the technology and so. And due to such advances, the company had planned on ending its milk delivering business but kept that very last route open for the sake of Mr. Woodrow's love and pride for his job, and the owners being the bleeding hearts they were, couldn't find the words to deny the man his happiness in his end days. Now, while on it I may as well mention that *Doc Proctor's Dairy* delivered more than just milk, on notice they would also bring cream, butter, cheese and all sorts of diary products, but the times were changing and there was no more money to be had. Sad kinda... So, I had to disguise myself as there was no more milk delivery after the death of Mr. Woodrow. Luckily for me, this wasn't common knowledge. And Mrs. Waters, the widow, was known to be a sort of shut-in, so my assumption was most of her town news came from those who stopped by her home on business, such as the dear dead Milkman and the Mailman.

Unluckily for me, all twelve of my rivals also knew this, and all twelve of my rivals also had the same idea. I'm not gonna get into any arguments here about their chosen fake identities, it happened and no matter how much I could bitch and whine, it would all remain the same. So there is no point in that, but what I will say is... twelve Milkmen, that's reasonable, but thirteen, that's just damned ridiculous. It seemed that to us, the chance of a lifetime came about with the death of a good man, and though it may be a little lowdown for us to take that as our opening, we were also none of us not the type to let such a chance pass bye. With no time to spare, knowing that with twelve other men on the prowl, we each set out as soon as we each learned the news. What happened when one Milkman ran into another Milkman, now that is where the real anecdote begins.

I was in my uniform, white slacks and shirt, black rimmed hat with black shoes and matching bowtie, a six-pack of chilled milk glasses dangling from my hand when I rounded the corner to see Chuck Charles, Brian Crowther, Bentley Lee and Jack Speegle approach the unsuspecting widow, Mrs. Waters' house all at the same time, all from different angles, all in the same Milkman uniform I wore. When they saw one another, an argument broke out, some shouting ensued and soon those glass bottles full of milk began flying through the air. I ducked behind a wooden, whitewashed fence and watched the chaos from a peephole.

Brian Crowther went down first, catching a bottle directly in the face. He hit the ground like a wet sack and remained there the entirety, playing dead. Chuck Charles, now he was known for being one hell of a bare-knuckle boxer and a damn fine bar brawler as well. While the others tossed bottles, he set his six-pack down in a calm manor and slowly rolled up his sleeves. He went after Jack Speegle first, the smaller man not one known to back down from a fight himself, hurled his last bottle at Bentley Lee but before he could get both his fists up, was being pummeled by the callused knuckles of the boxer. It took exactly four punches for Jack to fall: a left jab to the jaw, a straight right lunge to the sternum, a left hook to the body and a right uppercut to end it. Jack Speegle fell to the ground, unconscious and bloody at the mouth. I was amazed at the speed at which the blows were delivered. 1,2,3,4 and he's down and out, a fury of punches delivered perfectly. This left Chuck with Bentley, who was also known around town to be quite the opponent, having served in the first World War, he wasn't one to quiver at the sight of another man, no matter how large and mean. They advanced on one another with their hands up, ready to go. They circled, looking for an opening and when they both grew impatient waiting for an opportunity, decided to open up with a right hook to the jaw. Both, at the same time, both throwing right hooks, both dropping their left hands and both connecting with bone-shaking hits.

Both men fell to the ground.

I heard the sound of sirens approaching and decided it would benefit me to come back once the situation was dealt with and the street was cleared.

Later that morning, it looked like I was about to have some luck. With no other men in sight I had just come to the gate of the widow, Mrs. Waters' property when a hollering came from behind me. A hand landed on my shoulder and spun me around, I ducked the right hand of Garry Staley and charged into his lower stomach with my shoulder, knocking him over. His bottles broke with the fall, he swore at me and grabbed one of the broken bottles and stood to face me. Grasping the glass like a blade, he thrust forward and I dodged each stab with a quickness I hadn't seen since a teenager. When I was about to resort to swinging my six-pack at him, a white uniform flew past me and tackled my attacker. It was Jeffery Lawson, a tall sonofa-bitch, he seemed to be holding the other man to the ground but when Staley began to flail his limbs from underneath, I noticed the blood pooling up beside them. Apparently, Lawson hadn't noticed the glass and had been stabbed when his body fell atop that of Staley's. The size of Lawson pinned my attacker to the ground, helpless. I abandoned the plan and began to run down the sidewalk away from the scene, I hid behind the fence I was used as cover only some time earlier.

From there I watched as the police showed up, the officers rolled Lawson off of Staley. They cuffed the smaller man and put him in the back of their cruiser. A black hearse appeared shortly for Lawson. From my hidden post, I waited. And when the cars pulled away and all seemed clear, I began back towards widow, Mrs. Waters' home.

I hadn't gone two feet when two men bumped into me, shouldering me to the side as one chased the other. Each man wore a Milkman uniform. When the man in the lead stopped and twirled around, swinging his six-pack of milk bottles as I had thought of doing just minutes ago, I noticed that it was Stephen Keene, his face full of adult acne, red with anger. His bottles crashed against the skull of the other man, who, when knocked stumbling backwards, I recognized as Ed White. None of the men being much for fighting, they stared at one another after the hit. And just as I thought Ed was going to advance, a car that had been creeping down the road sped up. The screeching of the tires caught the ears of Ed and Stephen and before they could assess their predicament, were flipping over the hood of an old Chrysler. Ed smacked the windshield before rolling over the roof of the car and I suppose this is when the hit and run went wrong for the driver, as he ran straight into a telephone pole and was ejected through the windshield. The car halted and Ray Little popped out through the glass and landed on the ground at my feet. His body crumpled up and his neck bent cockeyed when he hit the sidewalk. He died instantly. Blood and glass ruined his Milkman uniform.

I quickly sprinted back home where I sat, gathered myself

and seriously considered calling the whole thing off. With nine men dead or wounded, my head was full of the horrible sights I had witnessed and what horrible situations I could have been in and almost was part of. And then, with nine men out of the picture, I thought how my chances had only gotten better at gaining the hand of the widow, Mrs. Waters. With a new enthusiasm, I picked up my bottles and went out the door with my head held high and a grin on my face.

Jonathon Strand must have been in some sort of hiding earlier and seen me, because he was waiting outside my front door with a baseball bat. He got me right in the gut and I doubled over, almost dropping the milk glasses. He brought the bat down over my back and I dropped to the ground. Fortunately, the milk glasses fell on soft soil and not concrete, leaving them dirty but not broken. Jonathon must have thought that was the end of me, but when he began to walk away I reached out and caught his foot and yanked it backwards. He fell face first to the ground, his jaw taking the bulk of the impact. Taking a great inhale I lunged forward in a sort of crawling-walk like an ape and straddled him, sitting atop his back. I threw off his black rimmed hat and grabbed hold of his hair, then I bashed his face into the concrete of my walkway until my arm grew tired. I sat atop his back for a few minutes catching my breath from the beating I had just given one of my rivals and when I noticed his body didn't rise and fall with breaths, I stood and thumped my chest like the ape I had become and let loose a primal, animalistic scream.

I snatched the glass milk bottles from the lawn, rubbed

them clean on the dead man's uniform and then started back on with my plan to whisk away the widow, Mrs. Waters, in a whirlwind of an affair.

In my new found primordial mindset, the body of Mort King didn't even surprise me; I didn't jolt or loose a breath as I strutted down the sidewalk, stepping over his body without having to adjust my arrogant stride. To this day I don't know what happened to Mort, he wasn't bloody and his Milkman uniform wasn't dirty in the least. He simply seemed to have decided to take a nap on the sidewalk and never woke up. He wasn't one for physical altercations, a thin and frail man whose nose was almost always in a book and if it wasn't there it was up the ass-end of his boss down at the Department of Motor Vehicle offices. Perhaps he saw the scrape between Jonathon Strand and myself and fell down dead in horror at the sight of what destruction mankind could do, perhaps his heart couldn't take the message his brain sent down, shocking it with a *that could be me* scenario. (Which it rightly could have been.)

There I was, the cock of the walk, set to bedazzle my love interest and her bank account when I came upon the last of the twelve men, Shaun Thomas. He stood beside the gate at the fence of the widow, Mrs. Waters', staring straight ahead, down the walkway and up to the front door. Not even the sound of my clunky black shoes took his blank gaze off whatever it was that had his attention. When I got near, ready to throw my fists, I noticed what held him so tightly and it stopped me, stopped my cocky stride, stopped my primal mindset and stopped my eyes from blinking.

There, descending the porch steps in her Sunday Best was the widow, Mrs. Waters, arm interlocked with the arm of a slick-haired, pretty-boy. Guiding her down the steps, all suited up in his Sunday Best was Joe Barker, the goddamn, Mailman.

In disbelief, I stood silently next to my last rival and even backed up when the gate was opened. We, Shaun and I, backed up, mouths catching bugs and our eyes fixed on the couple, backed up, and watched as the Mailman stole our woman right out from under us. They must have been half-way down the block before I blinked. Needless to say, neither Shaun nor I saw any reason to assault one another and without sparing a word, we slumped our heads in defeat and went about our separate ways.

Twelve Milkmen, that's reasonable. Thirteen Milkmen, that's damned ridiculous. A Mailman, now that's just plain wrong.

THE STOMA LAUGHS LAST
Dustin LaValley

HER TONGUE SLIDES across my ear and nibbles on my lobe brief enough to cause a pleasurable pain before bringing her lips to the skin of my neck. Kiss after kiss she works her way down to my clavicle where a suckle turns into a bite. Delicate fingers circle my naval and work their way to my ribs, where they trace each bone and continue their upward journey as our lips meet—succulent flesh and wet saliva. My hands gripping her hips, I pull her atop my lower stomach, her hands move to my shoulders to brace herself as she leans forward and her head dips allowing long brunette hair to sway across my chest, tickling me and causing a slight chill. She bucks her hips, bringing her thighs in tight against my own as I place a light palm on her butt and begin to massage, simultaneously pinching a nipple between my thumb and index finger. She takes hold of the shaft of my penis and grips tightly, stroking. Favor moving to her clitoris I spread her labia with two fingers and please with the middle. My chest rises and I inhale deeply, she moans and angles her head to the side.

Another buck of the hips and I'm inside her, moist and warm. Slowly and gently we thrust into one another. Bending in, bringing her breast to my mouth I grip her nipple between teeth and flick my tongue up and down and she pants heavily, our thrusting growing evermore quick and hard. I release and she flicks her head back, hair flying free and for the first time I get a good look deep into her seductive brown eyes as she peers into my own through a seductive narrow stare.

My breathing becomes savage, she swivels her hips as we thrust and I reach around her. One arm pulls her down against me and the other tugs at a lock of hair, yanking her head back to the side so I can watch her expression as I finish inside her. One final thrust and I freeze, about to discharge -

The raucous clatter of my roommate choking on his own breath wakes me. I glance at the wall clock: 3:13AM.

Motherfucker! I scream in my head.

Stupid bastard filled his lungs with poison for over forty years, turning white walls yellow and pink lungs black and no doubt killing his family along with him, with each puff of each cigarette. His dysfunction waking me in the first few minutes of sleep I've experienced in three nights, since the surgery... Operation. Whatever the hell you call the removal of a colon.

It's August and the humidity has overtaken the air-conditioning, I lay naked with a white, bloodstained hospital sheet half covering my lower body. A dirty golden line of piss flows through my foley catheter and drips into its bag. I can feel the water-filled balloon trapped in my bladder, creating a dull ache to accompany the sharp pain of the tube rubbing against my tender urethra. I'm covered in a sticky glaze of perspiration, I smell horribly of body odor and, my cock is uncomfortably shrunken and stuck to my prickly balls. With a wooden backscratcher I flick the damp sheet farther off my body, uncovering my new friend: the stoma. My little pink buddy entrapped by a clear ostomy bag. Shit spilling almost constantly from its mouth.

Kind of like some doctors I know.

The surgeons warned me, every little detail printed and pushed under my nose to dissect and mentally ingest. But they never said shit about the itching. The itching! It's fucking horrible. Growing worse and worse the longer my mind stays on topic. I fidget and fuss and become angry and agitated.

I tear the adhesive strip painfully from my abdominal skin, ripping the Tupperware-like appliance from my body; exposing my little friend.

My nails dig into the wrinkled, pink skin and I scratch furiously. Digging harder, scratching faster. The fresh air hitting my stoma is like a drug: drowning out all mental comprehension, asking for more and more and more.

A nasty sharp pain sends my body into a quick convulsion. I stop scratching and throw my hands into the air. I now notice the blood coating my fingers and knuckles. Breathing hard, scared, I glance down at my stomach.

My little buddy is staring back at me, frowning, slick with blood, with a bit of bloody stool slipping from its mouth like drool. "What the fuck was that about?" it growls.

I stare wide-eyed, stupefied and motionless.

"You got a fuckin' problem? Keep staring asshole, it'll help mend this shit up."

"Wha-" I begin to say.

"I'm all you got left now and you try and kill me?"

"No." I say, "No, I was only…"

The stoma tilts to the side just a little, like it's cocking its head at me. "Guess what, asshole?" It pauses, sinks into itself, and then pushes out and sprays blood and shit onto my upper stomach. "You fucked up." It coughs, "Now I'm un-fuckin'-" the stoma begins to jerk back, hacking something from deep within, and shit slaps warm across my belly in a big goober of liquid. "Now I'm un-fuckin'-usable, you piece of shit!" it manages to say with blood spraying.

"What? Why?"

"Don't you fuckin' question me you goddamn idiot! You fucked me up, now I'm permanent."

I close my eyes for an exaggerated moment, "The doctors, surgeons, they said you'd only be… I'd only have an ostomy bag for two, three months."

"Yeah, yeah, unless you tear it—me all up to fuckin' shreds!"

It goes silent, leans back and, seems to be staring me down. I stare back, silent, and picture it wearing a paperboy cap with a stogie between clenched teeth and one eye squinting. "No one will like you anymore, nobody wants to be friends with a shit-bag." It speaks with a hint of superiority in its voice.

"What? Why wouldn't -"

It leans forward and shouts, "Forget about ever gettin' laid again!" It laughs, hard and loud. "Your life is ruined, buddy. You're already dead."

The catheter hurts like a bitch as I yank it out of my dick, the balloon contorting to the inside of my penis and popping out with a wet burst. Blood follows, pooling on the sheets, but I don't care. I slide the IV line out of the fold of my arm, a fine trickle of blood oozes down my forearm, but it doesn't bother me. With all my strength I stand, grow dizzy and feeling nauseas, but it doesn't stop me...

The hallways of the hospital are surprisingly deserted in the wee morning hour...

I stand on the roof, on the ledge, a trail of blood behind me and my little friend laughing as I consider the next step.

Walking point for the rest of us.

NATASHA
Dustin LaValley

I PULL ON long, dark curly hair arching her back with one hand and, as she moans I slide my free hand across glistening pale skin to cup her ample breast. Head bowed to the side, a lock of hair tight in my fist, her seductive brown eyes stare into mine half-open in ecstasy. The contact of her eyes pushes my carnal lust and I thrust evermore powerfully, her head bobs and she closes her eyes, biting down on her upper lip. Her moans have grown to a guttural squeal pulsating with each thrust.

I inhale and close my eyes…

Natasha grins behind her glass of wine, a sinister expression… the Emergency Medical Technician takes to one knee and bends forward turning his ear to my mouth… I'm freezing atop a metal slab as the coroner talks into a handheld recorder… a tearful step-mother places a hand on my head and says my name before patting my own hands that rest across my chest one on the other… pure darkness as thump after thump slams my casket… utter silence is broken by the scrape of metal from outside my entombment… Natasha grins behind a lantern as my eye's focus in the dim light six-feet down…

I exhale and open my eyes.

She is curled up in the sheets, her sweat-slick body glistening by the illumination of the bare red bulb dangling from the ceiling. I lean forward onto my hands and begin to crawl towards her until she raises her palm in a halting gesture. She shakes her head no and points to the opposite corner of the room, grinning.

Naked, I stand and shuffle to the darkness. My penis growing softer with each step until I find the figure in the dark corner, the excitement brings my unit quickly to full stature once again.

Cowering, gagged and tied at the wrists and ankles, her drug-induced subservience weakened by every second spent in the dark comes to an abrupt end as I move within sight. Together her arms flail, her legs kick and muffled screams plead for release. I bend to scoop her up and toss her over my shoulder, taking a few blows as I do so. An elbow hits my kidney and I blink exaggeratedly and expel a gasp...

She stands on the sidewalk amongst a throng of young women and a few young men disgusted as women underneath the overpass... we pull to the curve and I point to her... she leans in the passenger window to explain prices and I plunge the syringe into her arm... she is pulled through the window as the car pulls away, our situation unnoticed...

I'm huffing air as I drop the prostitute on the mattress where Natasha is perched on the tips of her toes, ready to pounce, saliva dripping from her lips. The thin skin on the abdomen tears away easily by feminine fingernails, intestine spilling out of the wound. A wet scream escapes the gag as Natasha plunges her mouth into the girl's exposed gut. Rabid, my wife devours the internal organs of the flailing, dying young woman. With the scene unfolding before me I step backwards, back into the darkness of the corner and take a seat to hug my legs with my arms and wait for the scraps Natasha tosses to me when she is good and full. A tear streaks down my cheek and my eyes begin to sting, I realize I haven't blinked since I delivered breakfast in bed and close my eyes...

Hand in hand I watch Natasha say "I do" in reply to "till death do you part"... sitting beside my beautiful new wife she squeezes my hand tight as the Oncologist reads to her the test results... bedridden and ever-thin I watch her body eat itself from the inside out... the grin on Natasha's emaciated face as I inject the toxic concoction during her intravenous therapy... the primal sex we had one month after her miraculous full recovery...

I sit silently and wait for scraps of life.

A MIDNIGHT DRIVE
Dustin LaValley

A MIDNIGHT DRIVE to sooth a rambling mind and air a constricted heart. South, to Albany; south past 1E I'm not slowing. New York City, wide awake I drive on. Surprisingly the New Jersey Turnpike isn't cramped at 6 a.m. and I find that the sun rising over storage units in Delaware is appeasing and scenic. Crossing into Maryland, I yawn—Baltimore, 65 miles. Drifting off 55B I spot a motel and find a room. I lie in bed at 10 a.m. and pop 20mgs of Ambien and 100mgs of Seroquil and stare at the ceiling for 2 hours. I wake moments after my eyes close, limbs and mind are dead. Alone, sick, scared and depressed... I'm tired; so very, very tired and alone in Bodymore Murderland.

FAIRYTALE ENDING
Dustin LaValley

ONCE UPON A leisurely hike, I came about two small children in the forest. Plump and pale were these twin siblings of opposite sex. Curiously, secretly, I watched their sticky hands pluck sweet gumdrops from a house of gingerbread and frosting. Through a window I spotted a pair of vile eyes stalking, extricating my curiosity into suspicion. "Run, children, run!" I warned, leaping from my hidden roost. "Run, for surely you have fallen prey to a cannibalistic ol' witch!" I quickened my approach as the door slid open, revealing a *come-hither* wave from a wrinkled hand. Stumbling forward I declared, "No children, for sure it is a trick upon your lives!" Ignorant glances they spared my alarm—as though unaware of my presence the children strolled bug-eyed into a tasty demise, stimulated by sugar-filled desires. Halting to a shut door, I became overwhelmed by the realization that one can forewarn but one can not forbid.

FOR HER, INSOMNIA
Dustin LaValley

SHE GRASPS MY hand as I point the remote towards the television and says, "I can't sleep without the noise." I free my hand and snuggle close to hold her beautiful nude body and kiss her neck.

And as I close my eyes for a sleepless night I can't help but wonder what demons wait for her in the silence.

HUMIDITY
Dustin LaValley

AT ELEVEN STORIES high the buzzing and dings are silent, the air is fresh and the sights are not quite stimulating. Still, the mind is fresh and bladder full and sleep is days away... The desert has coated the rental with a film of dust that will not be removed until it is returned or rain pours from the cloudless sky... A sheet of sweat instantly sticks to my flesh as I step from the car and under the sun... Three hours of pent-up urine stings as it flows... The dirt crunches beneath my twisted footfalls, stumbling sideways, the haze overtakes me and I collapse to the dirt and I come to realize this endless landscape is not the Mojave, it is Death Valley...

I-15
Dustin LaValley

PLAYING DEAD ON I-15 your head drones with the ramifications of a night filled by perverted affairs... The drinks came easy and free and the quarter slots emptied pockets half drained by hourly rated escorts... Playing dead on I-15, as anxious scavenger birds circle above your pathetic soul for the next semi to speed down the desert interstate...

SHEETS

Dustin LaValley

KNUCKLES RAP UPON the frame of the doorway – there are no closed
doors here, they are not allowed. "7 a.m., wake up time!" the
attendant hollers in to the room that houses a polite Englishman
of forty along with myself; young and frail from sleep deprivation
and stomach ailments. The knuckles rap louder and the voice
rises, repeating itself. I pull the sheet over my head and attempt
to ignore the noise… to mimic sleep for another fleeting moment
in hope that it will deliver the real article. The attendant enters
our room, his voice overpowers his footfalls, "7 a.m.," the sheet
is pulled away to uncover my face, "wake up time!" Moaning I
lean on my elbow and watch through tired, stinging eyes as the
large male attendant stands above the opposite bed. "7 a.m.," he
pulls away the sheet from the Englishman's face, "wake—"

Abrupt silence.

"Mr. James," the attendant says in a soft tone, "Mr. James?"
He gently shakes the man's shoulder, an arm falls and dangles
from the bedside, the head of Mr. Harold James falls to its side
to stare into my eyes. "Lord…" the attendant steps backwards
slowly, then turns and bursts into a sprint out of the room, down
the hallway to the nurse's station. I continue to gaze into the eyes

of my roommate for a brief instant before I roll onto my back and cover my face with the white sheet to mimic the real article.

SLEEPING
Dustin LaValley

SLEEPING, I SEE myself gray as a ghost, stranded on the outskirts of this perverse community in which I reside. Wondering where I have been for so long and why I have felt so ill for reasons I can't understand, nor will, nor would want to understand and, whether or not to awaken and allow myself to communicate these unconscious ambitions or continue to sleepwalk; stranded, gray as a ghost watching my dreams pass by.

SYMPATHY OR SELFISHNESS?
Dustin LaValley

HE SLUMPS HIS worn head on my lap, my legs crossed underneath me on the cold wooden floor. I stroke his head and I know he understands something is different this time. From my caress he can sense my sorrow and from his big chapped nose he can smell the concern upon my being. His eyes close for a moment and he yawns: a big bold mug with yellow teeth and black gums, a long dry tongue hoarse from thirst. And in this brief display of exhaustion I can't help but hope that tonight will be the night he passes.

TEMPER, RED AS HER LIPS
Dustin LaValley

IN HER ATTEMPTS to decode his vocalizations she turns a wrong corner and heads down a one-way street. Distracted, infuriated, regard is tossed out the window to settle amongst disbanded cigarette butts—mutual friends in theory though blatantly unsuspecting in appearance. Screaming women stuck in golden era cardigans and skirts lift children into their arms and sprint for the side-walk, escaping the danger within the street by mere moments. She stomps on the gas, gunning for an unseen victim, a hit-and-run on a purely anthropomorphic basis: A premeditated murder due to faulty foundations via instructions in a foreign language, misunderstood and guided by illustrations. Lost in her fervor the oncoming car is unseen and collides with a mighty force, crunching metal and shattering glass. She stumbles from the crash confused but unharmed, undaunted by the wail of the horn under the head of the departed innocence.

WINTER IN SEASON
Dustin LaValley

"IT'S SNOWING," SHE says. I peer out the window and agree. "What shall we do now?" Shaking my head I gesture indecision with a rise of my shoulders. "Sleep it off?" she suggests. Nodding, I crawl into bed and reach for her. "Cold hands!" she shivers at my touch. I let go, she rolls away, and I accept that winter has come in season, in body and in mind.

Note from the author:
This micro short concerns the mood disorder known as Seasonal Affective Disorder (SAD). It is a serious condition that occurs mostly in the winter months and, having loved someone with SAD, I must emphasize the importance of understanding and education.

THE ENCHANTED DILDO
Dustin LaValley

JACQUELINE STOMPED OUT of the shop, almost loosing her balance as she slammed the door behind her. Tiny lightening bolts scattered down the glass before it shattered into shimmering pieces. "Hey!" the man behind the counter called to her, "You'll be paying for that, you stupid cunt!"

She kept walking, ignoring the voice that called to her; wondering if the man realized she had stolen an item from the *Sex Shop*, she turned to see if he had begun after her. No, he hadn't.

She slowed her pace; a pleasant stroll underneath a dark autumn sky, claustrophobic stars twinkling in the absence of clouds. Rounding the corner into an alleyway—cutting short the distance between the strip and home—she reached inside her large faux-fur purse and pulled out the item she had lifted from the shop: a gigantic dildo, four inches round, fourteen inches long. *It's a fuckin' beast*, she thought to herself, a wicked smile curled her lips, *a huge fuckin' beast*. She slowed her pace to admire the magnificent craftsmanship of her new toy. She held it up into the moonlight and gawked in astonishment at the size of the veins on the plastic pecker.

That's when she heard the footsteps.

Jacqueline spun around, expecting to see the man from the shop. She hid the dildo behind her back and during that very gesture she noticed it wasn't who she had assumed it to be. Without warning, her dark-red lips were crushed by a man's fist. She fell backwards to the ground of bum piss and beer, landing on top of her giant dildo. A quick gasp of breath escaped from her bloodied mouth and she rolled onto her side as the attacker stepped closer. She would have yelled, shouted for help, but feared the noise would simply amount to more harm.

The man bent toward her, and as he did so, his eyeglasses slid down his sweaty nose and he subconsciously and mechanically pushed them back with an index finger.

She saw the split-second window of open opportunity and boldly twisted her torso, swinging the giant dildo at her attacker. The tip caught him in the jaw and knocked him backwards, stumbling, his head tilted to the side with a grimace upon his face. He stood silent and watched her get on her feet, in a notable stupor at the sight of what came in contact with his head, the enormous dildo. Once balanced, she swung again. She gripped her weapon like a baseball bat and swung for the bleachers, knocking her attacker to the ground with a powerful wallop to the temple.

The man attempted to defend himself from the repetitive blows to no avail. The endorphins running through Jacqueline gave no leeway to mercy. The strange chant he squeezed out between death-grunts enhanced her rage beyond red and during the chaos failed to observe the cerebrospinal fluid which found its way into the plastic urethra.

She hadn't noticed the generous amount of blood coating the piece until under the illumination of her apartment lights. Dark brown blood covered the whole head and shaft of the dildo, or as she had now come to calling it, "The Beast." She found scrubbing the blood almost as enthralling as the attack and, somewhat sensual in a way.

A swirl of gray smoke fluttered as she waved out the match. The room now lit by a single honeydew scented candle, she slipped her beautifully sculpted body between the bed sheets. Pimples of pleasure rose on her bare flesh as she stroked her inner thighs. She inserted two fingers between her lips and began to titillate herself in rhythmic repetitions. She moaned and began rubbing her clitoral nub with her free hand.

Suddenly, her head bobbed foreword off the pillow, as if it was pushed from behind. Her self-attentiveness ceased by to the surprise poke, he retrieved the rod from under the pillow and gave it a good look over, baffled. *How odd*, she thought, but shook quickly shook off the bemusement and put the toy to work. Steadily, slowly, she lowered herself onto it, crouching on her strong dancer legs atop the bed. Moans of pleasure and pain escaped her mouth and then, she screamed.

Within never before probed areas of her inner female workings, an outstanding forceful stretch broke deep tissue. The pain hastily subsided with a soothing warmth, which she could feel filling her cavity.

Blood.

A snap of sharp pain knocked her off balance to fall backwards. The Beast refused to bend and showed itself pushing against Jacqueline' abdominal wall. Shrieking, screaming, she attempted to pull it out, only to create greater aggravation. Aggravation that seemed to provoke a series of changes, it grew thicker and longer. Pushing itself deeper and farther inside her until it chocked up her esophagus, up her throat. It pumped, knocking her head into the headboard with each pulsation. She held on, fighting though failing in freeing herself, growing weaker with each thrust. Eventually she let go of hope, lost her fight and closed her eyes in exhaustion. When it finished, its red juice filled her, dripped down her buttocks and limply decreased back into initial mass as like a human penis, flaccid.

Her eyes opened and fluttered once before she bled out, the victim of a dildo enchanted by a malicious entity.

Alberto woke up, sore but alive. It felt as if he'd been beaten all about the body, his insides like mush. Wiping blood from his mouth, he stared at the glob of blood and spit on the back of his hand, his petite, thin, hand with red-tipped fingernails. As his eyes cleared and focused, he raised his head with some effort and glanced down at his body. Besides the blood, he looked all right. In fact, he looked more than all right, he looked fucking hot. His breasts large and firm with perfectly circular areolas and small nipples, his stomach thin but not too thin, his thighs looked strong like a dancer's and where they met, a very short, dark colored landing strip of pubic hair led to his vulva, which he assumed had seen better days. He sat up, groaning through the pain, his throat coarse. Long, curly brunette hair tickled his shoulders, falling back as he rose. Fingering the hair he extended his arm, the strands of hair falling from between his fingers at its length. It felt smooth, silky. And when the last strand of hair fell against his chest, he saw the dildo. Stiff, large and bloody it sat between his legs. He let himself fall back atop the pillow and began laughing and though it hurt like hell, each huff scratching his esophagus and each puff bringing a sharp cramp to his stomach, he continued to laugh and he felt more than certain he was going to enjoy his new body.

HUMAN NATURE
Dustin LaValley

"WALLET, MOTHERFUCKER! NOW," the Pitbull spat as he jabbed the gun into the middle of my spine, wrenching my head back with a fistful of hair.

"Back right pocket," I said. "Take it."

He released my hair, "Don't you fuckin' move, motherfucker!" The pressure of the gun lifted from my back as he rifled through my pocket and snatched the wallet. "Don't fuckin' move!" He shouted, "Move an' I'll blow yer fuckin' brains out!" Once his footfalls were out of earshot I turned around. My assailant was gone, disappeared in the dark back alleys of the city.

I began towards the main drag, mentally listing the contents of my wallet and repeating the description of the Pitbull for reference when I found a Police Officer.

Turning the corner I ran into a crowd flowing down the sidewalk, snakes in suits slithered past, rambling incoherently into their cell phones; gorillas growled in doorways of Men's clubs, egging on passersby to wander to the back of the club; AlleyCats scavenging through dumpsters, scratching at the bugs in their ragged beards; Lionesses carrying cubs in their powerful jaws.

I pushed through the crowd, zigzagging and bumping shoulders. Neon lights buzzed and cracked, illuminating the sights in a stimulating radiance. In the busy strip I found it difficult to see past the heads surrounding me, the glow of the lights clouding the spaces between them. I stepped into the street, to be sideswiped by a cab.

The tires screeched and the car came to an abrupt stop and jerk; throwing me five, six feet from its bumper. I lay on the pavement in a daze, my eyes fluttered as the driver's door opened and the feet of the driver stomped towards me. "Fuckin' idiot! Look what you did to my cab!" The Weasel screamed at me, "Look, look what you did!" He pointed to the lump in the hood. "Look! Look!"

Horns honked and voices swore.

I stood with some trouble, tossing my arms to the sides as I caught my balance awkwardly as if drunk. Silent, I stared at the cab, at the imprint of my torso. The Weasel continued to scream, his head leaning towards me and his arm out to the side pointing, "Look, fuckin' idiot! Look!" I sighed and began to walk down the side of the road, in the gutter. The farther I walked the more the screaming faded.

Dazed and tattered, I opted for home to telephone the police about the mugging, as the more distance I covered the more I found the cliché to be more than a cliché. Stepping atop the curb I glanced at my options: continue down the crowed strip or cut down the alley behind Pickles Pub and catch a shorter route. The alley was dark and dangerous, though so was the strip as I had just learned… and what are the chances of being mugged twice in one night?

My face bounced off the muscular chest of the Pitbull as I rounded the corner to the alley. The laughter that emitted from his mouth was deep and throaty. He shoved me against the brick. "Long time no see!" he laughed, "You got any spare holdin' out from me?" He took a step forward and reached for me; my neck, my shoulder, my hair I know not as before he reached me I snatched his advancing wrist and yanked him forward and downward, straight into the palm of my hand shouting upward.

The crunch of jawbone and teeth caused my spine to shudder. He crumbled to the ground and I struggled to keep hold of his arm. He lay breathing shallow, eyes blinking long and exaggerated, his leg twitching. I stared blankly at his face. Through the pain he managed to speak, blood spilling from the side of his mangled mouth, "You... motherfucker... I'm... I'm..."

With both hands grabbing hold of his arm I pulled up with all my strength, raising his ribs and shoulder off the ground and stomped, breaking his arm from its socket. He screamed in pain. Letting his arm drop I bent to search his pockets. He didn't attempt to speak, if he did, it was hidden within the moans and screams bursting through bubbles of blood and snot.

From the pocket of his pants I withdrew a wallet, my wallet, and placed it in my back right pocket. From his waist I withdrew the gun and placed it against his forehead...

The walk home was pleasant and peaceful, a sense of pride inflating me and with the gun tucked between my belt and the flesh of my back, I felt different... dangerous. The most dangerous motherfucking animal on the street.

HONK AN BONK
Dustin LaValley

"THAT WAS DRUGSHOW with their hit 'Bass Be B-Bopin' for all you rush-hour pranksters out their thumpin' bumpers an' bumpin' dumpers. This is Hazmat Harry comin' at cha for the 5 o'clock slam an' cram, *Honk an' Bonk Hour*. And as always I have my partner in crime with me along for the ride; the man your father warned all you pretty-boys about, Carl the Crank."

"Fuck you, Harry."

"Luckily for us he found his pills. Where'd ya find your pills this time Carl? Inside one of the chin-roles of that prostitute from last night?"

"Nah, inside your mother's cunt, Harry... Ha! Mothers cunt, Harry. Get it? Ahahaha! Your mother's hairy cunt."

"You're a goddamn magician with words, Carl. If David Blaine and Ron Jeremy had a homosexual affair – and I assume Blaine would be the bitch in this one – and pooped out a little shit of a bastard son, it be you. Congratulations."

"Hey, while we're talkin' about kids why don't you tell everyone about that chick you thought was twenty-one?"

"Man, why you gotta bust me open like that, these people don't need to—"

"Nah, nah Harry. You're not bustin' my balls without a flick to your own. Tell 'em, go on, go ahead—"

"You're a real fucker, you know that?"

"Yeah, fuck you too. Now go on and tell 'em, 'cause if you don't *I* will and you know you don't want that."

"All right, all right fine you prick."

"Here we go people, a little romantic poetry straight from the soul from Mr. Hazmat Harry to your bleeding hearts."

"All right, now… See I'll tell ya best I can but unless you're me and were wearin' my shoes, you won't understand but since you're my listeners and I love you, I'll try my best to reiterate this sexual encounter turn legal litigation and entertain. As is my job now isn't it."

"Get to it, pedophile."

"Hey! Fuck you, Carl. I'm gettin' to it, just givin' a little background story, it's what us in the biz call foreshadowing… I think. I don't fuckin' know."

"Come on, man."

"See, I was at this party at my buddies' place and I see this girl, tall, thin, perfect high and tight ass and these tits… I swear they were like two completely circular melons stuffed in that dress and goddamn if they tasted fruity but anyway I see this girl standin' there with a drink in her hand and I move in all the while thinking to myself, *Hey, she's drinking so she must be at least twenty-one, right*? We hit it off, I'm all Rico Suave and the next minute she's draggin' me by the arm through the crowd—"

"Oh, shit. Hate to cut you off in the middle of your statutory rape reflection but we got our first caller."

"Guess you could say I was saved by the blinkin' light, huh?"

"You're a douchebag, Harry. Answer the call."

"Caller you're on the air with Hazmat Harry and Carl the Crank on the *Honk an' Bonk Hour*. What's your name, where you from, is your man adequately satisfyin' your urges?"

"Oh my god! Oh god! Please, oh god you gotta help us we're trapped under the 87 overpass on Dicks Ave. Please, oh god—"

"Whoa! Lady, slow down you're makin' me limp here. I can see both Carl's hands above the counter, that's not a good sign. What's this about '*Dicks*'?"

"Please, call the police! We can't get through. Oh god, please you gotta help us! My husband, he's hurt bad. There's so much blood! Please, oh plea—"

"Wow! Ladies, please refrain from making calls when you're paddlin' down the red river. Wow… *craazzyy*! Carl, you're takin' the next call I gotta punch myself in the balls to counter that pain."

"Looks like I'm going in, Captain. We got us another call, bright blinkin' red light and all."

"You got this one, bro?"

"Only for you, babe. You owe—"

"Jesus! You see that? All the lines popped up red. People, we're only two men… well, I can only speak for myself here. I can't speak for Carl, neither can his ex-wife I here."

"Hey!"

"No worries, man, no need to get all angry it's over be-

tween Bertha and me, no need for that... No need. Now answer
one of these calls you taint-licker."

"All right, here goes nothin'. Caller you're on the air with
Hazmat Harry and Carl the—"

"They're everywhere. These... these things are swarming
us their claws... One clawed me I'm hurt bad. It had wings, this
creature, one of those creatures from the sinkholes—"

"Harry, Harry I think your wife just attacked this guy. Ha!"

"It was one of those winged creatures it clawed me, my
chest, I'm bleeding you gotta get help I can't reach anyone the
lines are down or disconnected or something you gotta help me
I'm bleeding bad—"

"My wife is dead, Carl."

"They're everywhere, oh god... Oh god! It's coming
back... Shit! Oh shit it's coming back it's coming back, oh—"

"Oh... Christ, man. I didn't know... When?"

"Please, oh shit oh please help me it's back oh no, no, no,
no. Stay away! No! Please, let me live, no!"

"Last night, she was impaled right in front of me. One of
those, those demon things impaled her... "

"Well, Harry... Man I'm sorry... But hey, that's one more
hole than before if you know what I mean!"

"Already there, man. Beat ya to it you sick fuck."

"Hello? Hello? Sounds like we lost our caller, ladies and
men in ladies attire."

"We're on a role here, seems to be the day of the wackos.
But I'm not complainin', it's good for ratings and hell, the cra-
zier the better in my view."

"Fit right in here on the *Honk an' Bonk Hour*! So keep your calls comin' dear luscious listeners."

"Here we go again, caller you're on the air with Hazmat Harry and Carl the Crank, chillin' and a little bit of illin' on the *Honk an'*—"

"Gonna have to end that one premature like a crackhead pregnancy, Harry. We got a report from the Traffic Chopper for all you road-roids out there so listen up, here's your travel update live from the Traffic Chopper."

"Harry, Carl! Are you all right?"

"Uh, yeah..."

"Yup."

"Oh man, it's a fucking war zone out here. Stay in the studio, it's goddamn fucking madness. These creatures, they're everywhere. The roads are gridlocked with scorched cars and bodies... Mangled bodies, picked limb from limb."

"So you're sayin' to expect delays?"

"Goddamn, it Harry! I'm not fuckin' joking around here! Stay inside! These things are demons, they're pouring out of the sinkholes like hornets from a hive. They fly, some have wings, big giant wings with claws and others... There appear to be others on the ground, bipod creatures slick with some sort of... Slime some sort of goo-like substance—"

"I think Carl already beat you to the goo substance, it's all over his shirt and pants, there appears to be some crusted next to his lips as well."

"I'm not fucking playing around with you, goddamn it! This is fucking serious, stop fucking around! These creatures, these demons, they're ripping people apart. I can hear them screaming, I can see them being torn apart. Oh god... We're out numbered there are so many, they're everywhere literally everywhere. Oh no, oh no, shit! Oh fuck! Oh Shit! They're attacking the helicopter. Shit!"

"'*Get to da choppa*!'"

"Ha! Harry zinged, ya!"

"What the fuck! What the – Holy mother of god what the hell – It's huge, oh my god, its giant... Three, four stories high. Holy shit! It swung at us! The tentacles are as big as buses! This thing, this giant squid creature is attacking the helicopter with its tentacles... Fuck! Jesus fuck! It swung again, oh god it's gonna hit us, oh god, oh shit... Oh... Oh no! Oh fu—"

"Hey, you there? Hello? Traffic Chopper?"

"'*Get to da choppa*!'"

"Harry, it seems as though we lost the Traffic Chopper."

"I... I think a... Perhaps a moment of silence is in order for our downed comrades. Let's, you listeners out there take a moment with us and let's put Robbie and Charlie of the *Honk an' Bonk Hour* Traffic Chopper in our thoughts... Ah, damn it, Carl! That fuckin' smells. What you eat this morning, your grandmother's ass?"

"Whew! Wow! Even I'm surprised on that one! And no, no I didn't eat my 'grandmother's ass,' you cock... It must be that rotten vagina I ate last night, your wife's rotten vagina!"

"My wife is dead, Carl... I just told you that."

"Must have been why it was rotten, huh!?"

"Ahaha! Carl, as I said, you're a magician with words.

Let's head back to the phone lines. Caller, you're on the air with Hazmat Harry and Carl the Crank on the *Honk an' Bonk Hour*! What's your name, where you from, is your—"

"Please! Please don't hang up we need help! Oh god please help us!"

ROUND
2

AND IN THIS CORNER...

John Edward Lawson

I HAVE ALWAYS been a writer, dating back to early childhood. It wasn't until I hit 25 years of age that I decided to make a go of being an *author*, though, and there's quite a difference between the two things. As a writer one need only possess pen and paper, create whatever fictions amuse them, at whatever pace one is comfortable with. As an author, however, one must bow to the demands of the market—meaning the interests of advertisers and editors, not necessarily those of readers—at breakneck speed.

For those reasons authors tend to work only in one field, or write under their own name in a single field anyway, because they are "branded." From the outset of my career I was concerned about being painted into a corner, permitted to pursue only one narrative style, one genre. My idea was to write in as many fields as humanly possible from the get-go in order to point to an established track record in more than one area, allowing me to execute whatever story type entertained me. To a certain degree I've achieved success with this tactic.

For an author to be able to follow whatever creative impulse arises as would a writer, well, I have to think that author is pretty lucky. That's the case with me.

And then there's jokers like Dustin LaValley who think they can go around doing whatever they want. Not because they're authors, writers, or whatever, but because they are martial arts masters who could kill more zombies with their bare hands than some guy equipped with a chainsaw hand and shotgun. Bullies, to be polite. Sure, they'll whine about people like me just to distract from their own strong-arm tactics. If you fall for such cheap redirection techniques there's nothing I can do for you.

If you're a free thinker then I welcome you. We're going on a fairly grim ride. Humorous at times, nauseating at others, and hopefully entertaining, but most of all grim. If you like such stories you can thank me by challenging your local martial arts master.

In critical but stable condition,
John E. Lawson

THE LIGHTNESS OF BEING
John Edward Lawson

THE WIND SCREAMS through splintered rib cages and hollowed skulls, singing a vivisectionist's song. Beetles and spiders are barely audible, chittering in the background, battling for scraps under the cover of darkness. A hint of crimson stains the air; the sun's first rays are stabbing over the horizon. As the seeping flow of light warms the land the resulting convection mutates the very air itself into a violent-minded creature, lashing everything that huddles close against the sheltering Mother Earth.

In the dim light his worst fears are confirmed...his limbs are indeed bound. *They* stand in mute vigil over his prone form, a towering conclave of ill intent. His appeals to reason, to mercy, are muffled by the severing of his vocal chords, the excruciating removal of his tongue. This meaty sacrifice is offered up to the dread lord *They* worship: the Twin Snakes carried aloft by feathered devil wings. The double-helix serpent demands this tissue, this and more, for their two Promethean stomachs are never full.

Pliers are used to extract his nails; although he is bound, there is deep gratification for *Them* in this act—perhaps the symbolism figures in the arcane ritualism of their fetishised insanity. Next his teeth are extracted, the bloody protest of his gums ignored, and those that are too difficult are simply chiseled out.

The sun's radiant hatefulness pierces his eyes, stapled open to observe the tragedy that is his body. For *They* have only just begun, and the day is still young...

THE RIB SPECIALIST
John Edward Lawson

MY BROTHER WAS a cat. No, it's true. This is according to the Surgeon General of the United States of America, that master of the human anatomy. The only reason I'm thinking about any of this is because I happen to be sitting down to a good rib dinner. Ribs remind me of baby bro every time.

"Did I ever mention, doctor, that you inspired me to pursue a career in medicine?" Oh, but how rude of me to indulge in conversation about myself while neglecting the needs of my guest. I attentively supply a straw, with a host's perfected grin. Really, I probably should have read the thirst in his eyes minutes ago.

"Read any good books lately doctor?" I ask, continuing to sharpen the carving knife. "I surely have. Take Taddio and colleagues as an example. In *Behavioral Pediatrics*—1984 I do believe—it was revealed that their study showed, and I quote, 'permanent psychological damage inflicted on infants subjected to unanesthetised penile reduction surgery.' Well now, what do you think about that? They went on to add, 'it is both instructive and frightening that the severe and unalleviable pain of circumcision permanently alters the neural pathways in an adverse fashion.' I realize, of course, that this is not your area of expertise. Please, don't let me bore you with the findings of circumcision studies…"

not that I eat cats or anything SO WHAT IF I DID

The carving knife pierces the meat before me; it slices through the bloody-raw flesh with ease. I take my time to savor the sensation. It occurs to me that in the state of California it is a misdemeanor to eat either a cat or a dog, but we aren't in California. Of course, I realize this would be a poor topic to bring up at the dinner table. It dwells in my mind regardless. What would the good Dr. Sturgis have to say about that law? My brother who would have been mentally retarded, physically disabled, I wonder if he would have any insight to share with us about eating felines?

"I hope you don't mind the table-side grilling. These things are supposed to be all the rage up north." Let's see…that one patty of meat is starting to finally cook through. Curses! A little spot of grease just popped and landed on my therapeusis of internal diseases. Ah, well. That's what I get for reading at the table.

What I really want to say is: around the world cats are skinned and grilled, made into "pussy-tail stew," the recipes are endless. In parts of Asia it is considered the healthiest meat available to man. Several French and Italian squirrel and rabbit recipes are known for their ability to substitute cat meat as well. Ah, such thoughts!

"As it turns out, infants undergoing surgery may actually experience more pain than an adult receiving the same procedure, as the systems we have in place to reduce overwhelming agony are not fully developed in newborns. Interesting, no? Okay, okay, enough about work already. Sorry, I just can't get my mind off the subject. So, how are the kids doctor? They well? I understand your son is a rare talent on the piano. Maybe one day I'll get to cook for him too, what do you say to that? Don't have any family, myself, no. Our chosen profession can be somewhat of a hindrance in that arena. Had a brother once, though…"

My little brother, tortured to death twenty-five years ago today…a quake of rage surges through me, then subsides. "You know, I ought to clear up something. When I said earlier that you were the influence on my becoming a doctor, well, that much was true. It was actually my brother who made me decide to take up cardiology as my specialty, though. You see, he underwent open-heart surgery. Don't you remember, Sturgis? Or is it okay if I call you Richard. Richie then. Thought I'd mentioned all this before now. About my brother, that is. Aha! I see you eying these ribs. Feeling hungry yet?" I'm not used to carving the ribs directly from the animal but sometimes in life you have to improvise. "You ever eat cat? Oh, come now sir, don't give me that look. I only ask out of curiosity. Certainly I am in no position to judge!"

My brother. The surgeons cut him open from his sternum all the way around to the center of his back. Then the murderous assemblage of medicine's best and brightest pried back his ribs like thieves at a bothersome door, all for a clear shot at several hours' worth of organ abuse. I should really loosen up and think about something else.

Cats, the world's great hunters. The largest, the tigers, I

have studied numerous accounts of them acquiring a taste for human flesh. Once they cross that line the only recourse is to hunt them down and kill them. It becomes an addiction with them. They just can't resist the easy, weak, smaller meat floating around defenseless in this world. There's no twelve-step program for such addictions, no, maybe a twelve-round safari perhaps.

"Supposedly the meat is tender like chicken. Cat meat, that is. Really now, doctor. You cannot find the notion to be so horrible can you?" I wipe the fresh stream of tears from his face and adjust his straw through the tight aperture in his latex gag. I feel like telling him what an honor it is to entertain a former Surgeon General.

"Didn't you say once—in an interview I believe—that you would, on occasion, take stray cats in and experiment on them? As I said before, I'm not going to be judgmental about anything here. After all, you gave said felines the benefit of anesthesia, even if you advised medical professionals to forgo such measures when operating on babies." So, I stand corrected: my brother was lower than a cat, if you want to be technical about it. The benefit of anesthesia was withheld from him.

Twenty-five years. Martin, if you are watching this from somewhere on the other side, this dinner is for you.

Applying the mesquite grill sauce to the meat I state, "Never fear, doctor. Just a little flavoring, no matter what it looks like, it's not blood…congealed or otherwise. Obviously, you're the one providing that."

Sometimes I can't help thinking that if common house cats provide such a good meal, then surely a tiger must be a delicacy. Of course, tigers are difficult to kill…or capture. They're smart, powerful. Tranquilizer guns seem to do the trick nicely though. There was a time when skinning something bothered me, really it did. They say there's more than one way to skin a cat... well, I'm here to tell you there's more than ten.

"Again, recent research indicates that males who have been circumcised have a lower pain threshold than those left, ah, how can I put it delicately? 'Intact.' You never were circumcised, were you doc? No, no, I checked already. The supposition is that you will have a much higher threshold for pain before going into shock." The gleaming blade of the knife and cruel tines of the carving fork enter Sturgis' chest cavity yet again. With the ribcage stripped of muscle I can clearly observe his lungs fill and expand, catch a glimpse of the heart quickly beating, racing almost in time with my own. "Not that you have to worry. You've got a world-class cardiologist on hand to ensure that your heart doesn't give out. And, with the muscle paralytics in your IV drip, you won't be able to hurt yourself. So you may as well relax...and do try to enjoy the dinner."

Actionable Intelligence
John Edward Lawson

MOISTURE CONDENSES ON the pastel-colored cinderblock walls, mimicking the sweat collecting on Shane's brow. He sits at a table. The chair has been stripped of its cushion, so the metal frame bites into his thighs. He would stand but they threatened to beat him the last he tried it. The table itself is formica, well used. There are stains on the table. Dark stains.

The linoleum floor is light brown in color and in need of repair; some of the tiles are starting to buckle and peel. The florescent lights overhead buzz and flicker. He wonders if they're rigged like that to put you on edge. This used to be a classroom, after all.

Four others are in attendance. Three are guards in standard military garb, scattered around the room's perimeter; two male and one female. The fourth seems to be a doctor of some sort. He is sweating even more profusely than Shane, which can't be a good sign.

An official interrogator strides in, his uniform freshly dry-cleaned, followed by a female subordinate who looks unsure about her role here. The interrogator is cordial enough even while being cold as ice. He informs Shane that he's sorry about the delay and, when Shane complains about the chair, he flies into a rage. "I demand you find this man a proper chair to sit on!" Soon enough his commands are executed.

Shane begins to think perhaps there is a silver lining. Maybe it's all a mistake and he can reason with these people. "Please, where am I? Can I make a phone call?"

"Of course. But first you must do something for us. We want names."

Shane scrutinizes the interrogator, the doctor, the guards. This is serious. He's got no idea what they're trying to dig up but he has no intention of playing their game. "I don't know what you're talking about."

The interrogator becomes cross. Is this how he's to be repaid for giving Shane a comfortable chair to sit in? But despite his anger Shane doesn't budge. With a nod the subordinate interrogator orders the guards to restrain him. The doctor, shaking now, steps forward.

"We're going to get names, one way or another."

"Uh...uh..." Shane begins to hyperventilate when they pin his hands to the table and the doctor produces a bone saw. "Names! Okay, there's Glen Milford over on First Avenue. He's in on it!"

They all look at each other. The interrogator is pissed. "No. *We* want names. Got it?"

"You want names?"

The blade is placed at the first knuckle of his pinky finger, just below the fingernail.

"Jorge!"

"Jorge? Which one of us is supposed to be Jorge?"

Shane looks around, unsure. "Um…you?"

The interrogator's face contorts with rage. "Do I look like a fuckin' Jorge to you?!"

Before Shane can reply the saw bites into skin and bone. He still has six people to name and twenty-seven knuckles left to go.

FULL SERVICE PUMP
John Edward Lawson

IF THERE'S ONE thing Todd knows it's cars. Day in, day out he watches them at the pumps while he eats chips and puts away one soda after another. Brent told him that a 1972 Porsche 916 came zooming by the other day, but what does that punk know anyway? *Yeah right*, Todd tells himself, *a freakin' 916*...even so, he's kept his eyes peeled ever since Brent dropped that on him.

Not like he's bound to see much of anything interesting tonight. Just a few more hours and the boss will take over at 6 a.m. If Todd isn't asleep when the man shows up then it'll be a good night. The rows of gum and cigs are staring at him like he's done something wrong. After thinking about it he decides *what the heck*, starts shutting things down, and writes a "screw off" letter. He doesn't need this crap anymore.

That's when the '03 Lamborghini Murcielago pulls into the station. Todd knows this because he secretly keeps *Motor Trend* in his stash of *Hustler* and *Penthouse*. Whoever that is, they're sitting in a quarter million dollars worth of car. The vehicle glimmers under the uneven light of the station. The door slides up and out comes a sleek leg. *This is better than a wet dream*, he thinks as he watches the total babe stand and stretch in the cold night air. *Just wait 'til that dumbass Brent hears about this*!

Hastily Todd turns the booth lights back on, brushing crumbs and fast-food icing from his shirt. There's no way he's going to screw this up. Seeing that she looks a bit confused he rushes out, realizing she must be used to that full service stuff. "Good evening ma'am. Fill 'er up?"

She looks at him, then after a moment says, "Yes."

That smile on her face is kind of weird, almost like…Todd isn't sure. Can it be that she digs him? He reaches for the pump, feeling stoked, trying to think up some smooth talk, or at least some questions to fill the silence.

"Wait," she says, her hand warm on his. "Don't be so hasty."

"Uh, sure…" Todd can't make up his mind if he should be gawking at the incredible work of engineering or the cleavage spilling over this broad's low-cut front. In a second she's sliding her hand down the front of his pants and all he can think is, *Man, this is like some kind of porno*!

"You want to 'fill 'er up' don't you?" Todd just nods and licks his suddenly dry lips, swallows. She drags him over to the car, that strange smile of hers widening. Even with her working him, unbuttoning his filthy pants, he can't help stealing a glance at the beautiful vehicle.

"You like it?" she purrs.

"The Murcielago? You know it. This is my dream ride right here."

She chuckles at this for some reason. "You know what it means? In Spanish?" He shakes his head so she tells him. "Bat.

It means bat." A couple yanks at his waist expose him to the early morning air.

One nervous glance around doesn't reveal any witnesses. Whatever...he was going to quit anyway. Who cares if somebody catches him getting it on with some hot chick on top of a Lamborghini? In fact he *wishes* somebody would see them so he could prove it wasn't just fantasy. This is even better than the time that he set the pumps to five cents a gallon for his friends. Finally he gets it together enough to respond to her. "Bat huh? They can call it whatever they want. With 571 horsepower I'd buy it no matter what."

"Yeah, well, this one's had some modifications. Close your eyes." With a woman that looks like a model on her knees Todd isn't about to say no.

Afraid that he'll finish before the nameless hottie gets started he tries to focus on the make and model, the specifications. "Modifications?" He swallows, overwhelmed by the moist heat he's slipping into. "What kind of, uh, modifications?" He almost sneaks a little peek but he's gone too far to blow it now...no sense in scaring her off or something. The warmth keeps rising, almost to the point of burning, and the wet confines constrict painfully. Even Todd can tell by now that something is wrong.

When he opens his eyes he realizes that the crazy ho has stuck his johnson in the gas tank, not her mouth! "Lady, what—" but before he can finish it happens: a dozen, a hundred razor sharp, needle-thin fangs stab into him.

The woman stands back while Todd shrieks like a baby. Bored by the whole spectacle she lights one of those menthols he hates so much and studies her nails. Meanwhile, the steaming wet maw inside the car has begun to pulsate horribly, sucking the liquid life straight from the most vulnerable network of blood vessels Todd has to offer…his groin. In a matter of seconds, before he can even contemplate how get himself out of this, he has already lost too much blood to fight back.

"You're going to muss up my paint job!" the woman yells, batting his clawing hands away from the car. With the sudden influx of blood the tortured flesh caught in the entrance to the "gas tank" continues to expand, a boner of proportions beyond Todd's capabilities. He bursts open. The extreme pain almost doesn't register now as Todd withers, caves in, and is reduced to no more than a dry husk.

His corpse slumps to the ground and the woman brushes away the dust of his broken-off penis, then lovingly replaces the gas cap. Stepping over the shriveled remains she considers wiping down her windows, but when she sees the murky liquid this station tries to pass off as windshield cleaner she almost vomits. "Oh, *totally* disgusting!" After tripping on the corpse and cursing she gets back in her car and speeds away, going from zero to sixty in less than four seconds. Another satisfied customer.

CHORES
John Edward Lawson

DURING MY LAST visit with mother her deterioration reared its ugly head. When she offered coffee, I accepted even though, as a rule, she serves it nearly boiling. The coffee was served in a large soup bowl for some reason. Mother smiled; her affection was measured only in spoonfuls.

I did my best not to ask about coffee mugs, or to fixate on the dark blotch lurking under the steaming surface. Mother's words were lost on me in the minutes that followed...my attention was drawn by the realization that something alive was struggling in the creamy brown murk.

Roaches. Big ones that dwarfed the spiny free-range specimens in the field out back, with leathery wings batting helplessly and antennae shriveling in my scalding beverage. One's head broke the surface and it made an audible chirp, but Mother failed to notice.

I excused myself, and retrieved the fly swatter from her utensil drawer. From that distance I watched her staring at the wall behind my chair, still muttering, and acknowledged she hadn't been speaking to me to begin with. Then, when familiar forms began to shift and twitch under her loose skin, I turned in that flimsy swatter for a claw hammer, realizing the coffee wasn't my real problem after all.

THE SOLUTION
John Edward Lawson

HE LOVED THE breaking of backs more than anything else. An upright body was an affront and nothing more. "There are twenty-six vertebrae," he would bark into the shadows; blackouts were a regular occurrence.

On the subway, crammed in with other passengers like the sardonic thoughts in his head, he would scream, "Don't touch my coccyx!" Within seconds the others would leave a disturbed void around his person.

Often he lamented his inability to observe the contours of his spine. Mirrors lie. Secretly he only stole purses to smash the compacts carried within.

He took up yoga with the hopes that his neck would loosen up a bit, allow him a full view. His envy of Linda Blair boiled over more than once and she had to get a restraining order against him, but this was nothing new.

He tired to pay men at the gym to twist his head, just enough so he could see his back, make sure everything was in order. They stared at him, with their thick arms and suspicious minds. Eventually security started recognizing him and he had to stop. That's when he devised a contraption he could attach to his headboard, one that would assist in his quest. He stayed out later and later searching for the right parts, the necessary tools. His mother didn't bother to ask about this latest obsession, instead questioning him on whether or not he'd found a job. He declined to answer. Jobs were for the spineless.

The hare-lipped boy across the street served as his test subject. The boy's muffled screams were pleasing somehow. After two days bound in the basement, and several tries, he got the results he was after. He made sure the neighbor boy was never see again, all while maintaining the image of "good son"/ marginally insane son.

Eventually his mother discovered him when serving his daily cocoa. He lay belly down on his bed, topless, staring at her from between his shoulder blades. The frozen expression he wore was unfamiliar: it was that of contentment.

LURKIN'
John Edward Lawson

"SO WHA JOO do den, homes?"

"Ah done busted his *ass*, muhfucka."

"Busted da damn foo ass?"

"Word 'em up kid, split dat bitch's wig like a damn tricked-out, ho-ass *bitch*!"

"Good lookin' out mah nigga, but shee-it, ah can handle up on mah own biznus 'n shit."

"Ain't no thang. Da muhfucka done been owin' my ass fo' some bool-sheeit, naw mean?" The phone rings. Chauncy stops his tirade long enough to pick it up. "Jeeah?"

"Yes, may I please speak to the bitch of the house?"

Chauncy glances over at Kareem, who is lost in a reefer haze. "Wha da fuck?"

"Is this the bitch? Would that be you, ma'am?"

"Wha da fuckin' fuck?!" The line goes dead. "Ey! Ey!"

"Yo, chill one time. Wha da fuck be up wit dat?"

"Fuck!" Chauncy slams the phone down. Over the next few minutes they talk about past fights and sexual encounters, high school teachers they hate and strung out clients. The phone call's sting fades, not unlike a bad dream. Mindful of his parents downstairs Chauncy keeps the television at a relatively low level. It is, after all, 1:15 a.m.

The phone rings. Hoping it might be that superfly hottie he encountered at the park Chauncy snatches up the receiver. "Jeeah?"

"Hey, it's your mother's dick. I haven't been up your ass since last night and it's making me lonely."

"*Who the fuck is this, bitch*?!"

"Oh—oh junior—oh here it comes sonny boy—"

"Ah muhafuckin' *kill* yo ass, muhfucka! Ya fuckin' *hear* me?! Kill yo ass dead as *shit*, bitch!"

Laughter pours through the line just before the other party hangs up.

Kareem is checking him out. "Yo man, what it is? Ah be strapped like a *muhfucka*, jus' *say* da damn word."

"Shit. Da shit ain't shit. Jus' turn up da damn TV, foo."

Kareem does as asked. They pass the glaucoma reliever back and forth a few times. It occurs to Chauncy this is the anniversary of his cousin's death.

The phone rings. They both turn to observe it…that ringing is somewhat annoying, after all.

Kareem scratches his armpit. "Aint'cha gonna ansuh dat, muhfucka?"

"You do it, foo."

A battle of stares ensues, one Kareem loses. After answering the call he grunts a few times, then hands the phone to Chauncy. "Fo you, foo."

"Who it be?" Chauncy whispers.

"Some muhfucka. Sheeit! Take dat damn ting, ain't got all night 'n shit." There are medicinal herbs to get back to, after all. With a sigh of trepidation Chauncy takes the phone. "Jeeah?" "Ah! Oh junior! Here it be comin', oh yeah!" The offensive string of expletive deletives to explode from Chauncy's mouth only causes the caller to laugh. "That's right, you dumb thug bastard. I bet you're jumping up and down like a gorilla stuck in the zoo. Right? Right?" Chauncy begins to shout unintelligibly. "Want daddy's banana to suck on? Huh, gorilla boy?"

"Bitch, ah kill yo mama and yo mama's mama, an yo sistah and yo ho, bitch! An' ah'll fuck dem bitches too! Pee-Wee Herman pervert bitch!" Chauncy slams the phone down. A portion of the plastic cradle fractures and falls away.

Kareem appraises him with an unsure look. "Dude man, ya be dusted? Tha's some *fucked* up shit."

Ignoring these inane comments, Chauncy curses and kicks some CD's and fast food containers around. Then he hears the sound of his parents stirring downstairs. His shoulders sink and sweat clutters the terrain of his forehead. "Damn, man!"

"Chauncy!" his father bellows. "Chauncy Reginald Jones!" This outburst is followed by that familiar awkward, expectant silence.

Chauncy sighs and heads to the bedroom door. When his friend comments on his middle name, he lurches as if about to strike him. That shuts Kareem up. Chauncy sticks his head out into the dark corridor only to have his eyes assaulted by the lights moments later.

His parents are on the landing, faces creased by the agitation and bewilderment that can only be caused by interrupted sleep.

"Boy, what in the *world* is going on up here?!"

"Well—"

"And what did we tell you about that language? We won't be having that *damn* language in our home!"

"Okay—"

"This is a *Christian* home! Do you understand what I'm saying?!"

"Okay—"

"And no *good Christian* is up at this hour of the morning!"

"Well—"

"Now we already let you have that Kareem boy here overnight, don't be having your lowlife friends calling at all hours neither! The phone rings one more time and I'll tan your hide!"

"Okay—"

"Now get to sleep, boy, and stop fooling around!"

The lights go out before Chauncy can reply. His parents stomp down the stairs, muttering amongst themselves like conquering barbarians disturbed by bawling natives. The sweat has reached Chauncy's armpits now.

Back in the room Kareem is struggling to hold in his laughter. "*Damn* yo, ya done been *told*."

Chauncy just stops and stares, not even bothering with a verbal reply. Then he turns down the television a bit, takes his seat, and stews in his anger. Meanwhile, Kareem is drinking soda and laughing at the sitcoms. The situation endures in this state for the better part of an hour.

Then the phone rings.

Chauncy picks it up after a split second, not even allowing time for a complete ring. Without bothering to listen he places the receiver on a nearby stack of magazines. Did his parents hear? Thirty seconds later there's still no stomping or shouting, so all would appear to be well.

"Let's cruise."

Kareem nods; his car waits outside and they both need to blow off some steam. Chauncy takes his revolver with him, just in case. Both are packing condoms...again, just in case.

They drive pointlessly for quite some time. Langley Park holds no thrills, surprisingly, so they stalk through the neighborhoods. At one point they may or may not see a deer. Either way they spend half an hour driving around in circles hoping to shoot the thing. It would make for their first hunting trip. Sadly, venison is not in the cards and they continue on.

Up ahead is the intersection of Riggs and 49th. On the corner is a dilapidated gas station boasting an operational phone booth. Drawing closer now they observe a man in the booth.

"Yo yo yo...slow up...slow up dawg...be checkin' dis shit out."

"Wha da—? Word, niggah, dis foo done nutted up in dis here sumbitch."

Indeed, the white suburbanite is in the wrong. He stands in the booth waiting for someone to pick up their phone, blatantly masturbating all the while. Kareem and Chauncy look to each other, both having reached the same conclusion.

"Dis here foo need to get got."

"Sho nuff."

The car prowls up alongside the booth without drawing the white man's attention. Chauncy leans out the window, squeezing the trigger five times. Kareem floors it and whips around the corner, nearly ejecting his friend from the vehicle. As they argue, speeding to points unknown, the white man is crumpled in the shattered booth. Blood pools around fragmented glass.

Strangely, Chauncy never receives any prank phone calls after this.

INACCESS

John Edward Lawson

MARTIN FIGURED HE no longer needed the pistol because, he assured himself, he was officially dead. Just ask anyone, his family in particular. Take a look at the mantle, or the walls, or any of their dressers or desks at work. You wouldn't find evidence he existed, that was for sure. Not after eleven years in the inaccessability camp. Seventy-eight degrees south, ninety-six degrees east, seventy degrees below zero (Farenheit, mind you) and about a hundred degrees behind the ball.

No, no. Martin had agreed with himself this time. No more thinking about the past, no more dwelling on Polus Nedostupnosti. That was impossible! He was dwelling in a somewhat comfy suburban home outside Chicago, not a Soviet science camp in Antarctica. The dog that Martin absently reached out to pet was in fact his own shadow, so he returned his hand to the keyboard. He'd served his time, right? He'd spent eleven years of his prime stuck in some God-foreseaken Soviet-era scientific camp trying to extract as much vital information as he could, just like the goverment wanted. All those long years he'd dreamt of the hero's return home. Instead he was snuck into the country just to live in his parents' converted attic.

"Don't you worry any now, son," Martin's father had told him. "We'll make every effort to get you back up on your feet. You have our word." Instead, the house had become an inaccessability camp of a different sort.

During those long polarized nights dread had come to conquer him. It wasn't supposed to conquer his parents, no, just him.

"Did they treat you well, dear?" It had taken a week for Martin's mother to get up the nerve to ask him that inane question.

Instead of answering he withdrew further into the haven he imagined the attic would provide. His room had become an inaccessability chamber.

Looking at the bottom of the bottle he was drinking from gave Martin a clear view of the words, "Pet is 100% recyclable." This was enough to disturb his next two days so much that he could not remember them. Let it suffice to say he erred on the side of loyalty and did not recycle his shadow.

All the years he had sacrificed in that sub-zero Russian nightmare. Even the scientists who really were from the former Soviet republics stayed only a maximum of eighteen months.

One night he crept up on the ledge by the shakey ladder that descended to the rest of the house. Without a doubt his parents were discussing the "possibility of sending him back there." How could they send him back to Antarctica to spy on Russian scientific research? Only the United States government had the means or authority to execute such a plan. He wanted to tell them as much. Instead, he found his tongue had become no more than an inaccessability ramp into the cordoned-off confines of his skull.

The memory of white moving with a life of its own was petrifying; a small army of men dressed in white waited for his return. Facing the fact that his parents had betrayed him Martin decided it was finally time to put his shadow to sleep.

DUMPSTER BOY

John Edward Lawson

THE BOY LIVED in a dumpster, and Laura wanted to know why. It had to be dangerous living there, of course, due to the fact garbage trucks emptied the containers on a regular basis. It was more than just concern for his welfare, though. She observed him from afar over the course of several weeks, and somehow the refuse disposal trucks always managed to miss his domicile. She never ceased to be amazed by their oversight. Eventually she had to take a closer look.

On especially nasty summer days the raunchy stench wafted up to Laura's office window, nauseating her when she left it open. It was August 10 when she finally forced herself to leave the sterile indoor environment. Stylish sunglasses protected her eyes against the glaring white industrial buildings, but nothing could mask that tangy odor. She almost turned back twice. This sort of thing had never happened while she was in college, that was for sure.

Just when she was losing her nerve she became aware of feral eyes peering through a gap in a heap of rubbish. When she called out the flush of embarrassment stung; there was no reply. The eyes retreated. A hunched form skittered away.

Seagulls had flown in from somewhere, circling overhead, their shadows screaming over broken desks and rotting food. With the way the sun was beating down on her Laura decided to complete her excursion another day.

Alfonso was lost in yet another account from his honeymoon travels. While he busied himself with regaling Laura and Ginny with his Tahiti tales, the boy was constructing something just outside his dumpster. Some kind of refuse Easter Island, by the looks of it. It disturbed Laura's concentration to have Alfonso prattling on, to hear Ginny's absurd giggles.

What was Ginny doing in Laura's office, anyway? The woman had a sixth sense for how to perturb people. And what was with her street-casual wear? Everybody in the company knew that smart-casual was the bare minimum dress code. Laura suspected that Alfonso would have continued with his report to her if Ginny hadn't wandered in with her formfitting denims.

"So there we were—"

"Oh, I can only imagine—"

"—stuck in the middle of—"

"—how terrible—

"—I mean really, it was just—"

"—I wish I'd been there to see your face—"

"I mean, you can just imagine—"

Who the hell was Alfonso's wife, anyway? Laura didn't recall ever seeing a photograph of the woman, or hearing her name mentioned. Not that it mattered. The subject weighing on her mind was whether or not the waste management firm was going to follow up this time. She had already left three anonymous messages regarding a vagrant in one of their trash dumpsters. They had yet to acknowledge her increasingly urgent recordings.

At least the boy was taking the parcels of food she left on a daily basis. For a while he had seemed especially malnourished, from a distance at least. Maybe she could get him healthy enough to take the beating waste management workers would surely dole out once they discovered him. For the time being nobody reported the gift baskets of assorted cheeses and candies that regularly dissappeared from the mail room.

Ginny was distractedly fondling Laura's framed diploma from Western University. "I bet you did some furious tanning when you were down there, huh Al?"

Laura grew a bit too uncomfortable. It had been three years, but the diploma still held power for her. "Ginny, uh, could you not get fingerprints on my diploma?"

"What?" the woman asked, becoming aware of what her hands were doing. She jerked her arms back suddenly, causing the frame to topple and shatter as it hit the floor.

Alfonso chuckled inappropriately. "You know, this reminds me of the time…"

As if the sixty-hour work weeks weren't enough…did the company really expect Laura to put up with this incompetence? Beyond the window seagulls cawed madly at the unforgiving sun.

"Are you sure it's not an animal?

"Of course it's a boy. I mean, I've seen him."

"Well maybe it's not a trash dumpster. Maybe it's—um—a ratty old trailer that's falling apart. Or something."

"No, no. No. It's for sure a trash dumpster. There's a whole bunch of them back a ways behind my office, and the garbage men always come and empty the rest. It's so…"

"Sad? Creepy?"

"Yeah, it's like that."

They sat in silence, trying unsuccessfully to ignore a lesbian couple arguing in the next booth. For some reason Valerie always insisted on meeting at the same place. Maybe next time Laura would force a change of rendezvous. In the meantime she simply felt sorry for the young guy sitting with the lesbians; he was squirming, trying to stay out of his friends' conflict.

"So…is he cute?"

"What?"

"Is he cute."

"No, God Val, he's only like eleven or something. I don't know, he lives in trash for Christ's sakes. What kind of question is that?"

"Just wondering."

"You can stop wondering any time."

"I bet he's got AIDS."

Laura choked on her drink. "What the hell are you talking about? Is something wrong with you tonight or what?"

"It's just that—"

"We're talking about a homeless preteen here. You think I would let him score or something? Is that what you think this is about?"

They stopped, realizing that the lesbians had halted their own argument to listen in. Deciding to call it a night, Valerie and Laura arranged to meet the following week at a new Italian place.

Laura took her time slinking onto the stage. "Stripper Concertina in B Minor" blared from the sound system. Right foot forward, step left, one two, one two. The top button of her business suit came undone and the howls began. Glancing over the top of her thick-rimmed glasses she could hardly discern the shapes moving in the the darkness beyond the stage lights. Worried that it would distract her she quickly focused on the remaining buttons.

A beer can hit the stage. Then another. Little hands waved dollar bills, feral eyes glared. Laura sank into something akin to the downward dog pose she'd learned in yoga class. She sank further into the pose, hoping the pinstriped slacks would hold together. Decayed Chinese food cartons rained onto the stage, followed by shredded documents and broken table legs. She really put her routine into high gear then.

It occurred to her that Valerie was probably waiting for her at that new Italian place on the other side of town. Her friend would understand though; Val knew how important it was for her to accumulate enough money to go to college. Maybe then she'd be able to get a square job and stop dancing for a living. It would be good to finally get away from backbiters like Ginny, or blowhards like Alfonso, whose hulking form was guarding the door.

A paper airplane folded from a twenty dollar bill whizzed past her upturned face. One two, one two. Feet spread as she bent over backwards, then rolled onto her side. The unwashed skin of the audience moved in unison, ragged clothes barely held together in the darkness. Another paper plane soared through the air, this one with a needle affixed to the front. It stabbed her abdomen.

"Hey guys," the DJ announced over the PA system. "Let's keep it clean."

Men not even old enough to drive held dollar bills in their mouths, praying, waiting. You couldn't have packed more of them in if you used a trash compactor. Laura called out, hoping against hope the music wouldn't drown her out. Somebody had to recognize the desperation lurking under her smile. The men began to grow impatient. The DJ kept an eye on the clock, knowing that closing time had to roll around eventually. Laura's ears remained trained on the audience.

They continued to wait.

SHOEGAZING
John Edward Lawson

HIS SHOES ARE black wing tips, polished to a dark mirror-shine.

They shuffle through mud and debris, full of sweat and fungus and odor.

He's very careful to avoid scuffing them—such a thing would ruin his pastime.

That's because he's discovered that during the day most of people out and about are women, especially on public transportation.

He is often thankful women earn less than men and can't afford cars.

This gives him the opportunity to stare at his shoes.

People think he is moderately deranged, what with his teensy-weensy steps and constant giggles among crowds.

The fact is he's attempting to avoid disturbing the surface of his shoes.

How else is he going to look up skirts and dresses?

In fact, he's recently upgraded to PVC faux leather, with a thick homemade coating of clear plastic to magnify things.

The holes cut in his pockets allow his seed to be absorbed by handkerchiefs.

He's all ready for the next seeding after spotting a pretty

young thing alone on the bus.

Standing next to her, sniffing his own scent, he pretends he hasn't noticed her at all.

The left foot inches over into place.

And, jackpot: she's not wearing panties.

Or, not jackpot: as he stares into the shadows where her legs meet...

...something stares back.

And when her stomach growls he knows it's not hunger.

Or, perhaps more frightening, it is.

Clotted blood drips onto his shoe, accompanied by the mauled hairless leg of a rodent.

When she turns and winks at him, he dives out the rear exit doors.

The bus is still in motion when this transpires.

As he prepares to hit the pavement amidst traffic he realizes his shoes are about to get scuffed, torn even, but he's probably going to be taking up a new hobby anyway.

THE BABY BURNS EASILY
John Edward Lawson

THE MACHINE BEGOT illness, absolved by autoerotic cannibalism. Flame on, flame off. Grime under the nails, specks of purpling flesh clinging to his forearms. Eyes twitching in their sockets, struggling to comprehend what they took in. Mastery of the flesh came in the form of a singular victory for the automations—erect worms thrust into the flaccid birth canal, creating a new species.

The baby was swaddled in the skins of failed flesh long forgotten; many more hung on hooks throughout the apartment, tanned by The Machine for the fun of it. No! Because evolution *demanded* it. The Earth was his burden, the future his progeny. His dominion would know no bounds. Shredded ligaments were used as dental floss, while hand-pulled muscle dried for thirty days under a heat lamp served as a tooth brush. The Machine had long since extracted his own rotting molars, hammered away the gap-toothed smile; nonuniform iron bits had been drilled into place, bolted into his dripping gums and splintered jaw. Stainless steel plates reinforced/reshaped the surrounding mouth, making the consumption of food a possibility once more. Every night he brushed the rust away only to see it return in the morning.

The baby was afraid of this new face. The face of the New

World, the rancid environment of Old World sensuous in the background. The planet continued to spin, no matter how many leeches The Machine fucked to death. He found one loitering behind a trash dumpster, feeding on an aborted fetus. The leech claimed to have served in Vietnam, claimed to be a war hero: The Machine's erect worms did the rest. In another room the baby cried ceaselessly.

Soon enough The Machine used medical scissors to snip the baby's vocal chords.

He was toughening the baby up, preparing it for the harshness of reality. Every time he held the cigarette lighter under the baby's foot it wasn't child abuse—it was an act of love. The Machine showed unrivaled tenderness to the baby, inseminating leeches trapped in another room to ensure that the baby had nothing but the choicest cuts to feed from...its own brothers and sisters.

"I christen thee, Simon!" The Machine bellowed one evening, smashing a champaign bottle over the infant.

By age three Simon showed much progress. He chewed off his tongue of his own accord, suggesting quite a lot of initiative on the toddler's part. The metal teeth suited him well. Self-cannibalism was enlightenment of the highest order, manifest in the flesh. Manifisted fuckhole leeches were bathed in a grime-coating of oil drained from vehicles three weeks dead. Simon was a beauty, yes, the eyes of the leeches said as much. That and more. Patches of charcoal-flesh were forming, bulbous mirrors of the world. A few more years of burn treatment and the baby should be ripe for mining.

Its umbilical cord had only kept The Machine going for one morning...The Machine was the first to admit that had been a bit of a disappointment. Its mother though, yes, her flesh fed The Machine for weeks. He relived the fond event, fucking a version 2.7 womb into the torso of a new leech every month, in which the baby Simon would be housed at night. Four weeks later mommy went down the gullet, gasoline and all.

This movie never could have a happy ending, could it? The Machine's film projector larynx cawed a midnight melody to robo-ravens weaned on bloodmilk from the breasts nailed weekly to the porch. They took flight and spread lice, spread West Nile Virus, spread his pragmatic mutations over great distances, dipping their sharpened beaks into honey pots tied to mattresses across the nation. Inebriated desires were bent into new designs for the purpose of cohabitation. Blood greased this machine, lubed the bored holes of his compatriots.

When the faithless began to wail in his work bay, The Machine would slip between their legs with a straw and suck down their broken water. The cistern of love overflowed on many occasions, clogged with malformed clumps of twitching red flesh, nets made of veins that convulsed around their premature catch. The grill never stopped frying as there was no shortage of consumables. Spleen milkshake with windshield washer: a delectable flambé on any day. Simon took his meals in the rear feeding hatch. Squeals of pain were the mode of communication used by father and son. The landlord was a screwhead, listless in the streets, used as a jackhole by the half-castes and pimps, teased by the screaming dogs licking their own hemorrhoids.

Prometheus sacrificed all so that we may enjoy these modern conveniences.

One day The Machine forgot to clean his hands after slathering motor oil in his hair and armpits and groin. Attempting to "toughen up" Simon with the lighter led to self-immolation. And Simon?

He had learned well indeed: The Machine was enough to feed Simon for months.

HUMANITARIAN
John Edward Lawson

THE THING SEX crime victims desire—more than anything—is for their partner to look at them the same way after disclosure of said crime, to remain desirable in the light of knowledge.

I know this because the eyes of my partners never frame me the same way after my own revelation.

Not Embeth. She's special, so I've kept her in the dark.

But tonight I'll make her feel the pain...masked, of course.

And tomorrow, when she sees I still love her despite what happened to her, that will be the greatest kindness she ever receives.

AX KILLER
John Edward Lawson

LESSON LEARNED: TOOL maintenance is essential.

Father spent his free time chopping firewood, more because mother was indoors than because we needed tinder.

Their inability to share rooms kept him too busy to notice his ax's blade loosening...until the last time he heaved back toward his shoulder and the blade went flying into his skull.

My free time is spent charging into hardware stores, slashing with my chainsaw, leaving mutilated blades and handles in my wake.

It consumes so much time that my only clue saw maintenance is overdue is the sound of the chain snapping when I raise—

THIS SHIT'LL PUT HAIR ON YOUR CHEST
(AND IN YOUR STAB WOUND)
John Edward Lawson

ME AND MY buddy Darnel were walking down the street when we saw a faggot.

Used the butt of my gun to bash his teeth in, then we took turns jamming our dingalings in his mouth.

"How ya like it *now*?" we asked...fuckin' faggot.

Blew off his legs at the knees and took turns painting his guts white.

Every day we find more and more faggots. It's at the point we don't got time for girlfriends.

Anyway, then we blew the faggot's head off, because the world don't need boys that does sex things with other boys.

FERAL
John Edward Lawson

OUR NEIGHBORHOOD WAS overrun by feral cats. Nothing kept them out of our yard.

Finally I resorted to sexing goats on a heap of razors.

Then, I drilled a hole in my boy's thigh, filled it with nitroglycerin, and blew that sumbitch.

Wifey was next. After staking her down I tied a scythe to the John Deere and plowed her field for the last time.

Our house was last on my list, burning after I filled it with molten demon seed from Satan's right nut, which he kindly loaned me for the evening.

Those cats never bothered my family again.

BREASTICLES
John Edward Lawson

TO SATISFY MY bet with Dustin I offered the woman at the bar, Mandy, $100 to let us examine her bazoombas.

Back in our hotel room we took turns feeling her up.

Seemed fake to me, but when Dustin licked and sucked Mandy's mammaries white milk spurted into his mouth. "Pay up, J-Law."

I dug my fingers into her knockers, pulling. A horrible tearing noise merged with Mandy's screams as the fake boobs ripped off in my hands, revealing a set of hairy, overripe testes on her chest.

There's nothing like being right.

And that white stuff Dustin drank wasn't milk.

THE FINGER
John Edward Lawson

IT HAD BEEN months since my finger was severed by a snowmobile. Just when I acclimated to my situation...

...a skier found my frozen finger. My doctors and parents convinced me to try reattachment.

It worked: my body accepted the flesh.

It didn't work: nauseating pain crippled me despite all treatments.

So I chopped off my hand...

...but they reattached it while I was unconscious.

The pain is ten times worse now, so bad they had to induce a coma for a while.

This time I'm chopping off the entire arm, somewhere nobody can find me...

MEDICAL INTERVENTION
John Edward Lawson

MITZI'S PARENTS WERE paralyzed by indecision. The specialists assured them her minimally conscious state was incurable.

Day after day they lingered in her hospital room, with the stench of antiseptics leeching into their clothes as Mitzi's head wounds healed.

Then a winged person appeared. In reply to their questions it said, "I come to answer your daughter's prayers."

Mitzi's parents smiled at their non-responsive daughter, then at the heavenly being.

After which it ripped out her heart.

The winged being disappeared as monitors alarmed and flat-lined, leaving Mitzi's parents to angrily ask her: "*How could you?!*"

LIKE WATER FOR SHAIVO
John Edward Lawson

THE NEWEST MEMBER of security here is Gopher. He has a criminal record, something of a bad one, but the hospice doesn't mind. In fact, they didn't even bother to look into the charges against him. Not when they're under siege from the media, from raving hordes bent on keeping The Living Dead Woman alive. Gopher is thankful to be at ground zero, to be a part of this. And maybe, just maybe, he'll get a chance to see The Living Dead Woman in the flesh before this is all over.

Patients who are relatively able-bodied spend time making Handbaskets of Joy to be delivered to sick and needy children around the world. The decorative handbaskets are piled up along one of the halls. Delivery people have been too afraid to come and pick them up with all the Bible-beaters outside.

That's where Reverend Humpty is inciting a mass of demonstrators. "They want to kill a woman even as she begs for water! That's right, my brothers and sisters, she still talks! I've seen the tapes the liberal media won't play! They were smuggled out by her nephew Timmy, who plays table tennis with her on a regular basis!"

This draws wails of horror from the crowd. One of them

carries a sign reading, *This has turned into a Jebacle*! Another reads, *Barbara, your sons have disgraced your womb! Cut it out with a rusty blade, bitch*! Another reads, *Anyone who isn't pro-life should die*!

And what is the message of Reverend Humpty?

"SOME-body is GO-ing to HELL-ll!"

His sermon draws cheers and amens and ratings for the corporate bullyboys. Speaking of corporate bullyboys, the good reverend's sponsor, Aqua-Aqua, arrives on the scene with an eighteen-wheeler loaded to the gills with water cooler refills and bottles in both Thirst-Ripper Size© and Bladder-Buster Size©. Aqua-Aqua's underlings distribute water to the masses—free, naturally—so that this one braindead woman might be saved. Never mind the drought victims around the world, or the Native Americans and the rust-colored tap water on their reservations.

Armed with bottles, jugs, and Super Soakers the crowd emits three cheers for the cameras. Then it is Reverend Humpty's moment to shine. "Who's with me, brothers and sisters? Now, I say now, is the time to storm the walls of Babylon!"

And why is that?

"Because SOME-body is GO-ing to HELL-ll!"

The demonstrators surge past barricades, shove reporters out of the way, pour through the front doors like the angry oceans, the oceans that spawned life—according to evolutionist heathen infidels, at least. The staff does their best to clear patients and grieving families out of the halls, to lock their rooms. Other staff members, bulked up by their mercenary security force, attempt to form a blockade. All manner of shouting, gesticulating, and threats are exchanged between the two sides.

Dr. Normandy, unable to take the racket any longer, storms out to confront the good reverend. When he asks them to leave peaceably Reverend Humpty insists that is no longer an option.

"Well," says the doctor, "You have to understand that you simply can't pour that water in my patient's mouth."

"Why?"

"It would be insane to do that."

"Do you hear, brothers and sisters? Those who follow JEE-sus are insane, according to this devil! And why oh why, Dr. Devil, would we be insane to carry out our holy duty?!"

"Because!"

"Because why?!"

"Because a person only ever has a feeding tube inserted after they no longer possess the ability to voluntarily swallow!"

"I'll tell you who won't swallow that: JEE-sus won't!"

"If you pour that water down her throat you'll asphyxiate her, you stupid fuck-asses!"

"JEE-sus have mercy on this sinner!"

"I'm still here, don't talk about me like I'm not!"

"You're here, yes, in the material world, while we—JEE-sus be praised—are working on the Heavenly plane!"

"Don't try to change the subject! The only way she can survive that water is with a feeding tube, and from where I sit I don't see one!"

"That's where you're wrong!" Saliva rockets from Reverend Humpty's mouth as he turns to the demonstrators. "Because, my brethren, let us not forget the living water and He who poured it!"

"Amen!" they shout in reply, so fervently that one of the patients expires.

Dr. Normandy pounds a fist into the palm of his other hand. "What the hell is that supposed to mean?!"

"The living water—*praise be*!—is a celestial feeding tube!"

"Amen!"

"Don't you folks listen to this fuck-ass!"

"Don't call me that!"

"What fuck-ass? Don't call you fuck-ass?"

"Call me Reverend Humpty!"

"And where's Deacon Dumpty, if I might ask?"

"He's a-dancin' on your grave, sinner!"

"Whoa! That doesn't sound too Christian!"

"The SPAW-wn of SAY-tan knows not what it MEE-ans to be a CHIRS-tian!"

"Christian?! I don't see any Christians here, Humpty-fucky!"

"Don't call me that!"

One of the nurses clears her throat, places a hand on Dr. Normandy's arm. "Um, don't you think—"

"Not now, Joan. Not when we're surrounded by a bunch of people who want to deprive a Christian woman from reaching Heaven at long last!"

"Oh! How dare you!"

"How dare I?! How dare I?! How dare you not believe that God will reward the innocent and punish the guilty! Don't you think he'll damn us to Hell?!'

"Yes! Of course! Praise JEE—"

"Then what's the problem, Dumpty-ass?! Why meddle here

if God has it under control?! Do you believe in God or not?!"

Since the argument isn't going so well Reverend Humpty resorts to speaking in tongues. Dr. Normandy laughs; the faithful take this as the sign. The sign from the Almighty, commanding them to raise up in this bee-otch. Chairs fly through the air and collide with volunteer craniums. Bottles of Aqua-Aqua crash through windows. Heaven-sapiens swing from light fixtures, crash into drywall, shout divine fuck-offs in what sounds like a mixture of turkey calls and the squealing of rodents copulating with ice picks. Pretty soon everyone is screaming in tongues, even the staff.

Several more patients expire in the chaos.

And, over the roar of unlawful combatants: "SOME-body is GO-ing to HELL-ll!"

The Handbaskets of Joy are trampled underfoot.

Gopher, having failed to join the rest of the security force, watches it all with clinical detachment. He knows this is the chance he has been waiting for. He slips into The Living Dead Woman's room. He checks her out while unlocking the wheels on her bed; there's still no sign of life. He runs, shoving her full-force through the hallways, ramming through the few protesters who have made it this far.

Meanwhile, Dr. Normandy has been sodomized with a fistful of uncapped syringes. Nurse Joan has been stabbed and trampled, her teeth pressed through her lips by excited feet, blood-burbling screams either unheard or ignored. Unsure who exactly The Living Dead Woman is the mob beats back family members and forcibly pours water into the mouths of any female they discover confined to a bed. They can't be too careful since the infidels might have disguised her.

Everyone is so preoccupied with the commotion inside that the area behind the hospice is deserted. The litter of demonstrators and reporters crunches underfoot as Gopher wheels The Living Dead Woman out to his van. After strapping her into a mattress anchored to the interior he hops in, puts the pedal to the metal and hits the open road. He knows a place where he can change out of his security uniform. While stopped there he can hook her up to the feeding machine he purchased on eBay—it's in the back, rattling around as they go over bumps in the road.

The doctors, the Christians, nobody is taking what he considers the perfect woman. After all, that criminal record of his was for necrophilia.

ABOUT THE AUTHORS

Dustin LaValley is the author of the collections *Lowlife Underdogs* and *Lawson Vs. LaValley* (with John Edward Lawson). He's had several screenplays produced with two in pre-production at this time. In the comic book world, he's the writer of a forthcoming thriller series and a series of short horror comics. Dustin is also a Sensei of Shito Ryu karate and studies Okinawan ju jutsu.

John Edward Lawson has published eight books and over four hundred works in anthologies, magazines, and literary journals worldwide. He is a Bram Stoker Award finalist and a winner of the Fiction International Emerging Writers Competition; other nominations include the Rhysling, the Dwarf Stars Award, and the Pushcart Prize. As a freelance editor he has worked for Raw Dog Screaming Press, Double Dragon Publishing, and National Lampoon among others, has edited seven anthologies, and served as editor-in-chief for *The Dream People*. He lives near Washington, DC with his wife and son.

CPSIA information can be obtained at www.ICGtesting.com
Printed in the USA
BVOW030403200213

313706BV00002B/7/P